Sorting It Out

Ellen Javernick

CONTENTS

Rigby

Harmful or Useful?

Who decided that a spider wasn't an insect and a porpoise wasn't a fish? Who decided to group things with the same qualities together? It all started thousands of years ago, when early human beings divided things into two groups. In one group were things that were useful to life, and in the other group were things that were harmful.

As time went on and people began to identify more qualities of things, they recognized different ways to sort and group them. This sorting and grouping process is called *classifying*.

Where and How Does It Exist?

Hundreds of years passed and the study of science evolved. Scientists, who by nature love sorting, wanted to come up with a more specific system for classifying things. Some tried separating things into the location in which they existed:

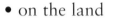

- on the land
- in the water
- in the air

The problem with this system was that some things could exist in all locations.

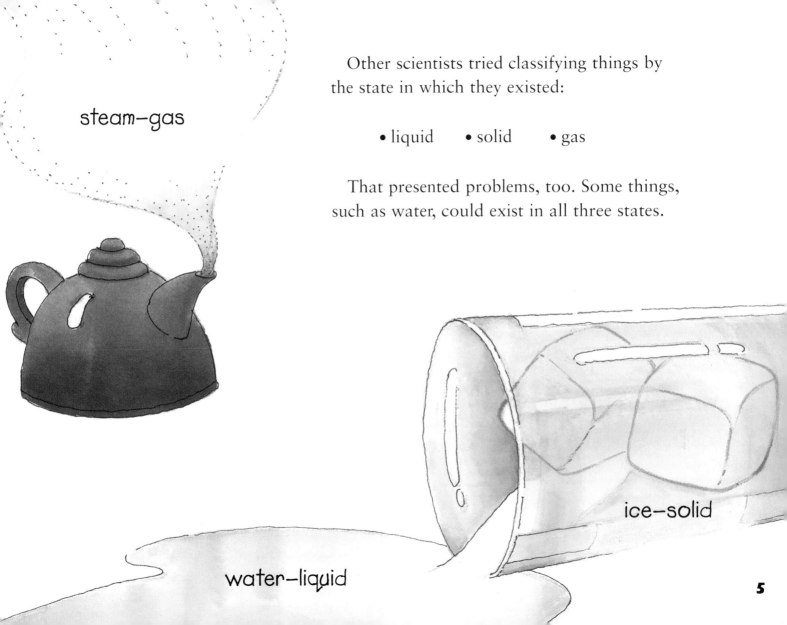

steam–gas

Other scientists tried classifying things by the state in which they existed:

- liquid   • solid   • gas

That presented problems, too. Some things, such as water, could exist in all three states.

ice–solid

water–liquid

Is It Living?

Scientists kept searching for a better way to
sort all the millions of different things in the
world. There was, after all, a world of difference
between a rabbit, a rosebush, and a rock.
Rabbits and rosebushes are alive. Rocks aren't.
That was it! Scientists began dividing the
world into two groups, living things
and nonliving things.

To distinguish living from nonliving things, scientists made a list of qualities for all living things.

Quality 1

• All living things, from an ant to a tree to a human, are made up of cells.

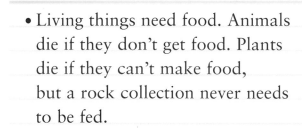

Quality 2

• Living things need food. Animals die if they don't get food. Plants die if they can't make food, but a rock collection never needs to be fed.

Quality 3

- All living things grow. Deer grow and daisies grow, but dirt doesn't grow. Plants grow in dirt, but the dirt itself doesn't grow.

- All living things reproduce. Animals have babies and plants have seeds, but you don't see boulder babies toddling around.

9

Plant or Animal?

Though pleased with themselves, the scientists weren't satisfied. They never are . . . that's why they're scientists. They wanted to sort the group of living things some more, so they divided living things into Plants and Animals.

Plants and animals differ in a number of ways. The biggest difference is that plants can make their own food. No, plants don't slave over a hot stove while animals order out. Instead, most plants use air, water, and sunlight to make food through a process called *photosynthesis*. Most plants eat only the food they make. A few plants, such as the Venus flytrap, also eat insects.

sunlight

water

air

water

Animals, on the other hand, cannot make their own food. They eat plants or smaller animals. That's why animals spend much of their time hunting for food.

Because plants are not constantly searching for food, they don't need the muscles and nerves and the five senses that animals have.

Although sunflowers don't have ears and eyes, they can sense where the sun is and turn to face it.

Instead of muscles, plants have roots that keep them in one place. The roots of a plant absorb water and minerals from the soil that the plant needs to grow. The roots of some plants grow for miles.

Plants keep growing all their lives. Some plants live only a short time and don't get very big, but some plants live thousands of years and are the oldest and tallest living things on Earth. The saguaro cactus often grows straight up for 50 years or so before it even starts shooting out branches.

25 ft. —

20 ft. —

15 ft. —

10 ft. —

5 ft. —

10 years   50 years   100 years

Plants grow bigger as well as taller. The trunk of General Sherman, a giant sequoia in California, is 79 feet around.

General Sherman is one of the oldest living things on Earth. It is between 2,200 and 2,500 years old.

GENERAL SHERMAN

Unlike plants, animals (that includes people) stop growing when they become adults. Most professional basketball players are over six and a half feet tall. Imagine how high basketball hoops would have to be if people never stopped growing.

Rosie ~
Age: 5 years

Happy
5th
Birthday

Different animals are full grown at different ages. Dogs and cats and most small animals are full grown in the first year or two of life. Larger animals grow a few more years. Giraffes, the tallest of animals at 15 to 18 feet, are usually full grown by their fifth birthdays. Humans grow at a slower rate than other animals. Most girls are as tall as they are going to get by 18. Many boys will grow for a few years longer.

Scientists decided to group all the plants together into what they call the Vegetable Kingdom and all the animals into the Animal Kingdom. You would think it would be pretty easy to tell members of the Animal and Vegetable Kingdoms apart, but it isn't always.

From a distance, this stick insect looks like just another twig.

The tawny frogmouth, an Australian bird, looks like a broken tree branch.

This looks like a fuzzy caterpillar of some kind, but it's really the bud of a pussy willow tree.

There is a lichen katydid in among the lichen. Can you tell which is the plant and which is the animal in this picture?

And what looks like
seaweed is really an
animal. It's a relative
of the starfish,
called a sea fan.

21

What's Left Over?

After scientists sorted living things into the Vegetable and Animal Kingdoms, they grouped all nonliving things into the Mineral Kingdom. This group is actually a classification of leftovers. Scientists struggled with this group for a while. The Greek philosopher, Empedocles, who lived about 2,500 years ago, tried to break all nonliving things into four subcategories:

- earth   • air   • fire   • water

The job of subdividing might have been just too much, because as legend has it, Empedocles leaped into the volcanic crater at the top of Mt. Etna. To this day, the Mineral Kingdom has remained undivided.

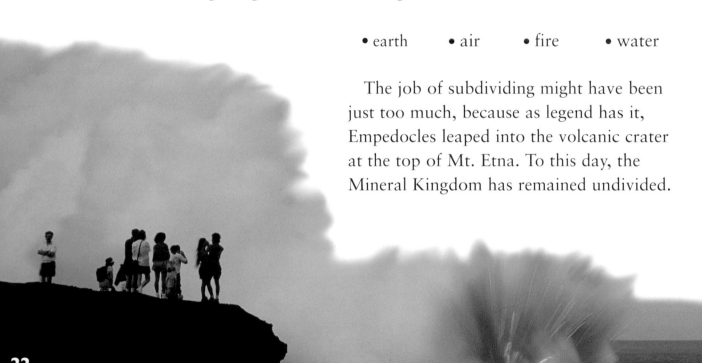

Separating living from nonliving things should be simple, but it isn't always so. Don't be tricked by the following:

These African stone plants are hard to spot because only the tips of their leaves show.

Watch out! There's a snake hidden in this sand.

Is this part of the human brain or a strange-looking stone? Neither. It's an animal called a brain coral.

Even under a microscope, these tiny mites look like specks of dust.

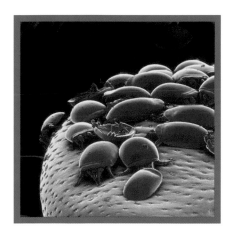

Does this belong to the Mineral Kingdom? It hasn't moved, grown, or eaten for months. No, it's a hibernating turtle.

What Was It Once?

What about the things that once lived but are no longer alive, or things that have been made from once-living things? Scientists usually say things that are no longer living are still part of the Animal Kingdom or the Vegetable Kingdom to which they originally belonged. They classify fossil fuels, like oil and coal, in the Vegetable Kingdom because they were once plants. A cotton shirt and paper belong to the Vegetable Kingdom, too. A leather wallet would be considered part of the Animal Kingdom. Do you know why?

What Is It?

Lots of things fall into more than one category. How would you classify these?

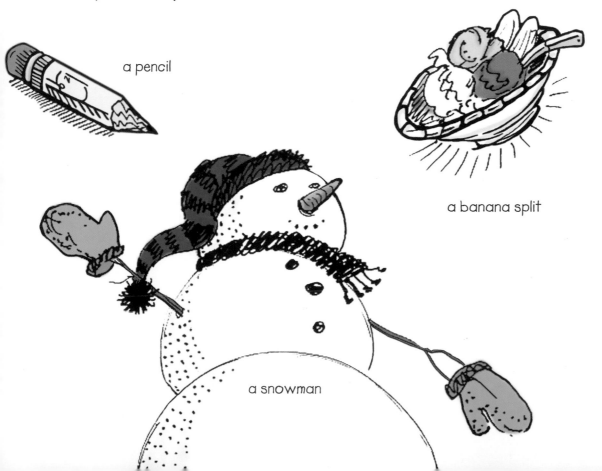

a pencil

a banana split

a snowman

What's the Next Step?

Once scientists worked out the three major kingdoms, they realized they could make smaller groups within each kingdom. This kept them busy for many more years. To start with, they divided the Animal Kingdom into two smaller groups: animals with backbones and animals without backbones. Then they took the group of animals with backbones and divided it some more. Here are five of the more common groups of animals with backbones:

Mammals:
warm-blooded and give birth to their young

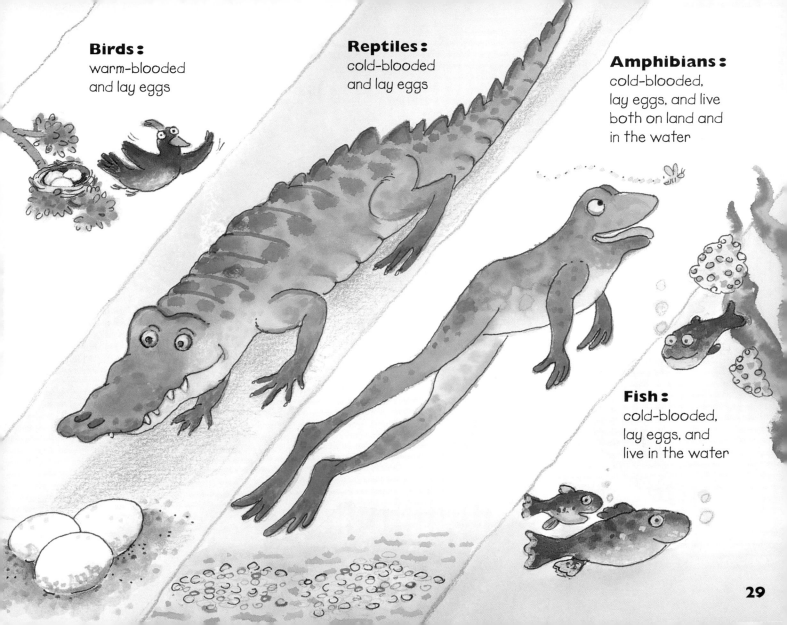

Birds: warm-blooded and lay eggs

Reptiles: cold-blooded and lay eggs

Amphibians: cold-blooded, lay eggs, and live both on land and in the water

Fish: cold-blooded, lay eggs, and live in the water

29

What's New?

And just when you think you've gotten the entire animal, vegetable, and mineral thing figured out, you find out that scientists have recently added three more kingdoms of living things:

- Fungi (mushrooms, breadmolds, and plant-like things that can't make their own food)
- Protista (tiny one-celled algae and protozoa)
- Monera (bacteria)

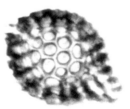

Protista

Monera

Fungi

But these new kingdoms will have to wait for another book.

Index